BLOOMSBURY PAPERBACKS

THIS BLOOMSBURY BOOK

BELONGS TO

Calum.

For Kevin -L.B.
For Mum and Dad, my inspiration -S.W.

BLOOMSBURY
CHILDREN'S
BOOKS

First published in Great Britain in 2000 by Bloomsbury Publishing Plc
38 Soho Square, London W1V 5DF
This paperback edition first published in 2001

A CIP catalogue record for this book is available from the British Library.
ISBN 0 7475 5013 1 (paperback)
ISBN 0 7475 4763 7 (hardback)

Designed by Dawn Apperley

Printed and bound by South China Printing Co.

3 5 7 9 10 8 6 4 2

Engines, Engines

Lisa Bruce and Stephen Waterhouse

BLOOMSBURY
CHILDREN'S
BOOKS

Have you ever been on a journey?
Riding on a train can be such fun.
There are lots of new and exciting things
to see. So step aboard the number engines
and let's travel together through the
far away land of India...

Engine, engine number ONE

Setting off in the midday sun

Engine, engine number TWO

Past the temple of Vishnu

Engine, engine number THREE

Women wearing bright sari

Engine, engine number FOUR

Chugging along the desert floor

Engine, engine number FIVE

Engine, engine number SIX

Naughty monkeys playing tricks

Engine, engine number SEVEN

The Himalayas reach up to heaven

Engine, engine number EIGHT

Past the palace with the golden gate

Engine, engine number NINE

Steaming down the Bombay line

Engine, engine number TEN

Follow the Ganges home again

The journey's finished, our fun is done

To travel again, go back to ONE!

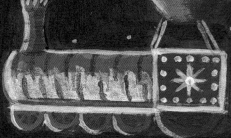

Acclaim for this book

'A richly colourful counting rhyme book set in the glorious surrounds of India,
with elegant elephants and camels, ornate temples and exotic native dancers,
in deep jewel colours' *Junior*